CHICKEN in the KITCHEN

by Tony Johnston
illustrated by Eleanor Taylor

SIMON & SCHUSTER BOOKS FOR YOUNG READERS
New York   London   Toronto   Sydney

SIMON & SCHUSTER BOOKS FOR YOUNG READERS
An imprint of Simon & Schuster Children's Publishing Division
1230 Avenue of the Americas, New York, New York 10020

Book design by Lucy Ruth Cummins
The text for this book is set in Cantoria MT.
The illustrations for this book are rendered in pencil and watercolor.

Manufactured in China
2 4 6 8 10 9 7 5 3 1
CIP data for this book is available from the Library of Congress.
ISBN 0-689-85641-5

For Lael: She never met a chicken she didn't like.—T. J.

For Lachlan xx—E. T.

There's a chicken in the kitchen,
and she's pokin' like the dickens

at the oven and the bread box.
Just a peckin' and a pickin'.

She is one right crazy chicken.
On the pots and pans she's wreakin'
pure-dee havoc, *pick-pick-pick*in'
like a set of false teeth clickin'.

Oh, that old cluck, she's gone peckin' everyplace, and I am thinkin'

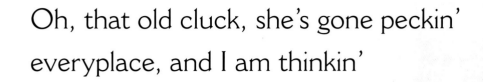

sure-as-Sunday she is starvin',
and she'll shrivel up and sicken.

Poor old biddy! Dear old chicken!
In a wink she will be stricken.
She'll desist her lively kickin'.
Her old hen heart will cease tickin'.

Well, I offer her some snackin',
but that pullet keeps on scratchin'
in the cupboards (where it's black), and
I'm forlorn. My heart is crackin'.

Then across the room I'm rushin'.

With my broom, I'm busy brushin'.

While my sweeper is a swishin',

dawns the plan for which
I'm wishin'.

So I chop the broom I'm flickin',
for a nest for my old chicken.

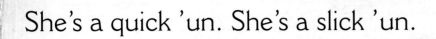

She's a quick 'un. She's a slick 'un.

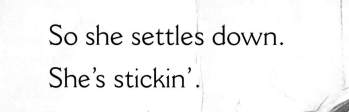

So she settles down.
She's stickin'.

There are eggs inside my kitchen

and they're hatching like the dickens.

Peep! Peep! Peep! How my heart quickens—

a whole
kitchen
full of
chickens!